D0901502

Curriculum Vitae

Also by Yoel Hoffmann
Available from New Directions

Bernhard

The Christ of Fish

The Heart Is Katmandu

Katschen & The Book of Joseph

The Shunra & The Schmetterling

יואל הופמן

Curriculum Vitae

YOEL HOFFMANN

Translated from the Hebrew by
PETER COLE

A NEW DIRECTIONS BOOK

Curriculum Vitae is published by arrangement with the Keter Publishing House and the Harris/Elon Agency of Israel.

Acknowledgements: Excerpts from this work first appeared in *Alligatorzine, Poetry*, and *Hebrew Writers on Writing*, edited by Peter Cole (Trinity University Press, 2008).

Design by Semadar Megged
First published as a New Directions Paperbook (NDP1145) in 2009.
Manufactured in the United States of America.
New Directions Books are printed on acid-free paper.
Published simultaneously in Canada by Penguin Books Canada Limited.

Library of Congress Cataloging-in-Publication Data:

Hoffmann, Yoel.
[Curriculum vitae. English.]
Curriculum vitae / by Yoel Hoffmann ; translated from the Hebrew by Peter Cole.
    p. cm.
"A New Directions Book."
ISBN 978-0-8112-1832-0 (paperbook)
I. Title.
PJ5054.H6319C8713 2009
892.4'36--dc22

                        2009019757

New Directions Books are published for James Laughlin
by New Directions Publishing Corporation
80 Eighth Avenue, New York 10011

Curriculum Vitae

[1]

My mother died on January 27, 1941. I was three and a half years old. When I was seven or eight, my father remarried and a little while later he asked me to call my stepmother "Mother."

My stepmother—Ursula—worked at an institution my father sent me to. The institution's director—Trude Tugenhaupt—had been my stepmother's friend back in Germany, and I remember (or they told me) that Trude's husband—Karl—died sitting behind the wheel and waiting for the light to change.

In time (after she'd become a widow) a worm entered Trude's body and, because of this worm, Trude entered various hospitals and was operated on (I think) two or three times. But the worm slipped away from the surgeons and eventually exited from her left eye.

The wedding, which took place at the institution, I recall only dimly. I remember that my mother (which is to say, Ursula) complained that a day before the wedding (or on the night before it) "a mouse jumped out from the blankets." I also remember that she said, "I made all the sandwiches by myself." While the guests were eating the sandwiches, the child Pinhas Indyk sat (I recall) on the balcony railing and swung a scarred leg before him.

Around that time (more or less) the event I've told of elsewhere occurred. While attendance was being taken at school (I was in the first or second grade), a dog mounted the stage and peed on the principal's leg.

After the wedding my father and mother rented a two-room apartment at number twenty-nine Rabbi Kook Street (which afterward became HaRo'eh Street) in Ramat Gan. My father was tall and my mother heavy and I never understood why they, who together weighed more than four-hundred pounds, slept in the same room, while I, who weighed less than fifty, for sure, had the other all to myself.

The landlord, Mr. Tziffer, lived in the opposite apartment. He was hard of hearing, and you could, if you walked behind him, curse him without his knowing it.

We lived on the second floor, and on the third floor (also with two parents) there lived a girl named Malka Shenwald, who, in time, would let me put my right hand between her legs.

What do I remember of those days? That the British had placed the city under curfew and that I asked a tall soldier who was wearing a red beret: "Curfew?" (I was very proud that I knew the word) and he answered, "Yes," and patted me on the head. I remember too that the janitor (who came to be called the custodian) at the school on the corner of Yahalom Street, Hayyim Eliyahu, who belonged to the Jewish Underground, urged the children to boycott English class ("the language of the oppressor") and the children happily complied. In the house across from us lived Mr. Rimalt, who later on became a delegate to the Knesset on behalf of the General Zionist Party. And there were always kittens in the courtyard.

[2]

In October, Pima the shoemaker asked me: Are you writing? I don't feel inspired, I told him; I'm waiting for the rain. Me too, he said. When the rain falls, the soles start to fray.

From time to time I write the opening of a story or a play and toss the manuscript into the waste basket. For instance:

A TRAGEDY

> Principal Characters:
> *Betta Marmor*
> *God*
> *Others*

I see dreams. A room at the airport and (Romanian) women who are silent. Or: The hindparts of a cow in a door and the door in a field. I sing (in my dream), *Sometimes I feel like a motherless child*, then go blind.

I dream that I'm a murderer. (Of a man? It was a kind of small mummy into whose neck I'd injected poison. But, without a doubt, there was life within it.) I try to wake up so I can find that I haven't killed a soul. I wake and understand that in fact I've committed a murder. In the morning, when I rise, I understand that I dreamed the part about waking up.

I see things: an old woman buying lungs (or brain). The butcher's name is Babayoff. The woman's name is Babayoff. The butcher has lungs (and a brain) of his own. The woman has lungs (and a brain) of her own.

Sometimes I see a person at the edge of the sidewalk or on the bus with a split lip or another ear. This person looks at me as though I were him. Or a woman (also a person) destined for me. But the distance in space is carved out between us and so it's impossible to reach her.

[3]

Because of that boycott of the English class my father moved me to a different school, in

Givatayim, and I had to walk three miles a day there and three miles a day back.

Vivian (we called her "Vivi"), whom I liked, went there too. Vivian's father (went the rumor), Mr. Siman-Tov, pursued her suitors while waving a house-slipper in his hand. Vivian herself liked, it seemed, Uri Hermelin, and people said that "she put out for him," though I didn't understand what she put out.

I imagine that the vice-principal (whose name now escapes me) is already dead, but then, in 1949 or '50, he confiscated notes that we passed around during class, primarily to learn from them who liked whom. Soccer balls flew in the air and the gym teacher, Yitzhak Nesher, who in time would become the oldest person ever to run around Mount Tabor, taught us to touch the tips of our toes.

I raised a wild pigeon. The pigeon got out of the crate I'd placed on the kitchen porch and came back to it. First it flew over the Urbachs' roof (their son, Micha, later became a psychologist) and afterward landed near the opposite porch where the widow Leikechmann fed her son Avremaleh (when he was seven Avremaleh drowned) with a

Mr. Siman-Tov pursued her suitors

teaspoon: This is for Aunt Blanca.... This is for Uncle Moshe.... This is for Mrs. Hoffmann....

[4]

There are things beyond belief, such as—that the German word for "feelings of inferiority" is *Minderwertigkeitsgefühle*. The earth comes from a dream and returns to that dream like my Uncle Ladislaus, who was made an honorary citizen of Ramat Gan. There was only a single asphalt road in the Ramat Gan of nineteen thirty seven, and he rode a donkey he'd received from the General Union of Hebrew Workers in the Land of Israel to his patients' homes. Also amazing, for instance, is that in Russian (or Polish) the word for God is *Bóg*.

Aharon Weiss, who taught Bible at the Givatayim elementary school, died twice. Once a rumor pronounced him dead and the second time it was nature. Most likely Bóg is responsible for both. He's also responsible for the chronic infection in Aharon Weiss's ear.

His Marxist orientation, on the other hand, Weiss arrived at against Bóg's better judgment (as Weiss saw it, the prophets were the proletariat's leaders), and whoever made trouble got listed in a black book.

Shimon Spector already had, most likely, some one hundred infractions against him noted in this black book, which our teacher Aharon Weiss forgot one day on the table during recess. Anyone who has seen the oil painting of the horde charging the Bastille (Delacroix?) would note, for certain, the resemblance between that picture and the eighth grade class as a whole, with Shimon Spector at its head (like the bare-breasted woman in that famous painting), tearing out the pages of the book one by one and tossing them into the air that autumn, like leaves, from the edge of the cliff at "the crater" (which is to say, the soccer stadium), toward the Ramat Gan team's goal.

[5]

Apropos the wild pigeon. Two years ago, in Cordoba, Spain I saw a sign:

PSICÓLOGOS CLÍNICOS
CENTRO DE ANÁLISIS Y
MODIFICACIÓN DE CONDUCTA

A man stepped out of a side door and said: *Qué perdistes ahí? Qué perdistes ahí?* (What are you looking for here?)—the tongue in his mouth smacking against the back of his teeth.

What could I have added? Was the sign for sale? Appetites are appetites, and we're all clinging with all our might to the thin crust around the earth.

Today, too, here and there I see such signs. Sometimes a gloomy person comes out of an opening like that in a building and most likely he's looking (like Romulus and Remus who founded Rome) for a she-wolf. Some of them change their old names for a new one just like Micha Urbach, the fat boy over whose roof my pigeon flew.

In the end, Vivian married an accountant and they probably did it in all sorts of places until she got divorced.

In those days (of sixth grade) I also liked Lotte. Lotte (whom Ursula had gotten to know

Sometimes a gloomy person comes out

back in Frankfurt) laughed two or three times regularly each hour.

Paul, Lotte's husband (a lawyer and notary public), had pink blotches on the back of his hand and I thought (mistakenly) that he had syphilis. When Lotte laughed, Paul's finger twitched and he looked to the side.

Lotte laughed when words like "pajamas" or "co-op committee" were uttered. A (rare in those days) bottle of raspberry juice made her laugh. A power outage. An overly large corset, and even the words (so long as they were said in Hebrew) "Do you have the time?"

Lotte's laugh is the nicest memorysound of my childhood. If she hadn't been twenty years older than me (flaming balls passed then from the eastern part of the Sharon plains toward the sea), I'd have married her.

I saw a man who'd peed in his pants. Maybe the world outside was too cold. Maybe something went wrong with the motion of the planets or in that head which is always found at the same distance from the earth.

After all, credit cards and I.D.s interfere with

our thinking. Why don't we fall onto the shop-keeper's neck as though he were our father in heaven? The white loaves of bread behind his back bear witness to a great conflagration.

[6]

Natan Schwabe's father had a shop in which he sold sausages and all sorts of coldcuts. Natan Schwabe himself slouched a lot and when we read Goethe's *Faust* aloud (in eleventh grade), Schwabe was given Mephistopheles' part.

All sorts of girls stood in the halls. The winter rains were absorbed by the wooden frames of the windows and the sociology teachers had a hard time getting them open. We knew (there was a rumor) that the principal Toni Halle's husband was a philosopher.

What did they call us? Usually Ya'akov Yampulsky.

On Mondays, in the gym, they made us jump over a crate they called a donkey. Some of us wound up breaking bones and were taken in a taxi to the clinic.

Schwabe was given Mephistopheles' part

Inside our leather bags sandwiches were crushed between history books and during the snack break the class smelled of eggs. There *were* dominant words (such as *"Comeoverhere"*), but on the whole information concerning empty space and time's direction they hid from us.

In the bathrooms, members were compared. Everything (houses, trees, street signs) made us think of girls. By the power of this eroticism, books read themselves.

As in the world of non-Euclidian geometry things came together. All inclined, as in a convex mirror, toward women's panties.

After our final exams we drank Carmel Mizrahi wine and rented a boat. Two girls whose names were Tsila sat in the stern. I remember that a fish jumped out of the water and we lost an oar.

We reached the place where the river merged with the salt water from the sea, and there, at twilight, among the purple shades, I knew: The world exists because of thirty-six righteous women (not men, as in the Jewish legend).

In 1956 we walked with a Czech rifle and an "elephant's pack" from the base at Beit Daraas to Kibbutz Gezer and back. Our leather shoes were stained with blood.

The following day, a soldier by the name of Bertonov (like the famous actor) fainted on the parade square and two others took him away on a stretcher. Afterward Bertonov announced that while he was "out" he'd come to understand Kant. The sensory impressions (so he said) derive from consciousness and so the world as a whole is him (that is, Bertonov).

On the Sabbath, my father Andreas and Ursula, my stepmother, brought an English cake and plum compote to Beit Daraas. Bertonov shook my father's hand and said "Bertonov." The sun stood directly over the tents and I suddenly understood that the two directions of time (forward and backward) extend to infinity and therefore the time people divide is entirely dream-like.

During the unit's march from Beit Shemesh to

while he was "out" he'd come to understand Kant

Jerusalem we bought an old donkey from an Arab (for ten liras) and tied our packs and rifles onto its back.

The donkey walked with us for two full days along the Burma Road and then, at the entrance to Jerusalem, we set it free but it followed us up to the library building at Givat Ram.

Fifty years have passed since then and the donkey, it stands to reason, is already dead. May he rest in peace.

We were about to head out on leave when Bertonov slipped and fell by the camp gate. At the hospital, in Ashkelon, they X-rayed his pelvis and found that a bone called the coccyx was broken.

We went to visit him and brought him chocolate and orange juice. Bertonov grabbed the handle over his head and pulled himself upward. We spoke with him about Sgt. Major Gantz and the punishment he'd meted out, and Bertonov said: It's good that I'm not there.

Clearly. Bertonov was where he was, and nowhere else. But Bertonov's ability to *think* of himself as being elsewhere filled us with amazement.

[8]

Now it's February two thousand and six and rain is coming down. Three-thirty in the morning. Dream matter's still in the air. An ancient Chinese woman. Hair for fertilizing lilies. The rest has been forgotten.

A man whose name is Van Hessen is responsible for respiration. Two girls attend to the joints and the ears. Someone (maybe a professor whose body tilts to the side) arranges the events of the past inside an enormous storeroom.

Who is driving time? Mr. Zaka'im?

An infinite number of books go out into the world (they're written by a woman in Tel Aviv), and in most the wife gets used to her husband in the end.

God's duty is to show compassion for all of this, for he is all-powerful.

In 1956, the knife belonging to the captain of frigate K 32 slipped against the steak on the plate (the festive meal took place in Palermo, Sicily, after the local authorities finally caved in and supplied the Jewish ship with fuel) and garden peas were sprayed onto the Italian officers' white uniforms.

When the Sicilian launderers hung the uniforms out to dry, the SS Miznak (the K 32) was already on her way to Sardinia, and from there to the west coast of Africa, where a school of dolphins escorted her into the port of Dakar. But the captain (whom we called Pincer Tooth) dreamed each night, until we reached the Cape of Good Hope, about the moment when the peas were sprayed. A thousand times he cut (in his dream) into the steak without any problem or at least said, with the proper accent, "Scusi."

That moment is called (in the history of the world) "the moment when the peas flew off the plate."

On the way to Djibouti, during a big storm, when even the cook lay helpless in his bunk and everything that wasn't tied down by ropes shattered against the opposite wall, the sailor De Lange made himself noodles and sang songs in Dutch.

After the storm, the water looked like a sheet of glass. We rinsed the vomit off the deck and gathered the broken pieces of furniture.

Pincer Tooth (the storm had driven the tragedy of the peas from his heart) moored the frigate to the pier and we went to look for whores.

In time, Knesset member Tamar Gozansky would say something (from the perspective of the Communist Party).

[9]

When we got to Sharm al-Sheikh, the only woman there—among some one thousand men—hugged me all evening long (I'll never forget that act of kindness).

We sat (I remember) under the demolished cannon. Ash that fell from my cigarette began to burn her jeans and a thin plume of smoke rose from them into the cold December air.

The kerosene lamps were lit (I recall) in the Egyptian prisoners' tents. At eleven, all at once, all the lights went out (and here the temptation grows very great to write something that ends with "stars").

Later we sailed to Eilat and there, on the pier, Joseph the carpenter waited.

He took the measurements of the pieces of furniture that had been broken during the storm and wrote the numbers in a notebook, and one could see how the god-like child came into the world.

I remember the girl (from sixth grade) whose name was Yemima. How we went to see "Ben Hur" together at the Rama Cinema and took shelter from the rain beneath a bookstore awning. There was a book there (I recall) about all kinds of soups, and a book about icons (which is to say, images of saints). Yemima, who was then, without a doubt, a virgin, held my hand all the way from Kofer HaYishuv to the end of Bailik Street.

In the Mickey Mouse cartoon before "Ben Hur" the cat's heart flew out of its body (it was attached by a spring) because of the love that the body has trouble containing.

In the end, the government sold to Ceylon the great bodies of iron that sailed the Atlantic Ocean.

The ships were already rusty and the prime minister there (her name was, I think, Bandaranaike) came to see them with an entourage of senior advisers.

This one, she said, we'll paint yellow. This one green. And this one, which I like best (so she said), red.

[10]

Our forefathers whose names were Samuel and Ephraim held the books of the Law to their heart. Some of them had opened the Holy Ark of the Law. Men among men.

From within the wealth of letters they knew the proper strategy, and were not afraid in enemy lands. On very cold days they covered the Sabbath dishes with their prayer shawls and called to the great Jew to descend from the heavens and walk among them as he is, tired and filthy.

Outpourings of the soul they knew. Broken hearts they knew. If trousers remained from that time, I'd hide my face in them.

All these dead rabbis. Arranged like threads of silk from the nadir to the zenith. They accompanied me in 1958 from Marseille to Paris and from there to Amsterdam.

From a textile merchant on the Place de

Clichy I received a janitor's room on the sixth floor, and in exchange for the room I promised to teach the sad boy on the fourth floor Hebrew.

Twice a week the boy put a café au lait and two warm croissants before me and I, in turn, by virtue of a tacit agreement between us, did *not* teach him.

Sometimes I went to Place Pigalle (nearby) and the whores called to me *Viens, viens.*

Two old women (whose names now escape me) baked me a cheesecake once a week and gave me what they called *chocolat* to drink.

I remember the woman in the Metro, at the Opéra Station, who hinted that I should follow her. She tossed her panties onto the burner in the kitchen, and the cross she removed from her neck she hung on the ... What do you call it? The clock's pendulum.

Each time she said *O cheri* the cross struck the wooden panels. To my amazement the wall clock kept on ticking, but there was without a doubt a distortion (perhaps from the shaking) in the movement of the two hands.

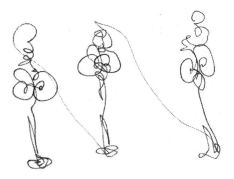

the whores called to me Viens, viens

[11]

In the halls of the Sorbonne the lights were low and the walls gave off a urinous scent. Words like *fondamentalement* were uttered there, or *en principe* or *procès dialectique*.

People sat on the surface of a planet that was burning within—all around it, in the astronomical distances, were other planets—and they spoke these words.

Later on, at cafés, within the scent of smoke, snug in corduroy jackets and wrapped in silk scarves, they waved hands in the air and said these words *again*. Because these words were *there*, like an aphrodisiac, countless bras and panties were shed.

I remember the man who taught philosophy. He was gaunt and would suddenly tilt his head (always to the left).

You need to understand, he would shout (he said *comprendre*), that Kant meant to say that a thing in itself is nothing.

Or when he spoke of Descartes: He didn't mean (his head tilts) that body and soul are *joined* in the pineal gland, but that they are *reflected* (*se réfléchissent*) in it.

Among the metal vendors and the office-supply store windows, every man longs for his mother. The gaunt man most likely had a gaunt mother, but she was *his* mother.

    Kyrie eleison. When will we stop all this wandering from house to house and person to person and word to word.

[12]

I saw corpses. I saw my grandfather Isaac Emerich's corpse. I saw the corpse of my Aunt Edith Forshner and the corpses of my father, Andreas, and of my stepmother, Ursula.

    Usually the mouth is open and the skin yellow. The body is, without a doubt, an empty shell. But where does everything go?

The sun stands over humanity by day and the moon by night. Whoever can, finds another body and lies beside it. Dreams fill us and when we're awake the things in actual space seem like dreams as well.

I remember the woman I married and how in Edinburgh we saw a cat devour a fledgling. How we drank soup in Munich. But what good is that soup we drank?

Kyrie Eleison. Just give us rolls and a clothes closet. Give us a single house slipper. The other you can hide beneath the bed. Give us a window we can open and close. Give us blotches on the back of the hand as we age.

[13]

On the train from Paris to Amsterdam Dutch children studied for an exam about Jeroboam, the king of Israel, and in Amsterdam itself I found a pension run by two homosexuals. When one went up the stairs the other went down them.

Bicycles were chained wherever you looked and what was above was reflected in the canals below. Old women peeked into the street by way of mirrors they'd hung on the wall, and some of them sat by the mirror all day, knitting.

Every so often a fat architect came out of a green door.

The telephone at the pension rang and the homosexual behind the desk said *kan niet verstaan* (I can't understand). A red-head came and spoke Dutch and through the window in the foyer you could see two children (like Max and Moritz, except that the latter have already been ground into meal).

Sometimes an ordinary moment is historical. Something happens. Tobacco falls. One changes the water in a vase. And he who gets it—gets it. Two days before Passover the chambermaid hugged me. She came from a small village (so she said) and no one there had ever suffered at Egyptian hands.

On the other hand, sometimes (during very hot years) water from the river that passed through the village would evaporate and entire families (among them also a Jew or two) would walk from one side of the village to the other, on dry land.

And the ten plagues as well. She showed me the boils on her lower back and when she spoke of God's anger, she crossed herself.

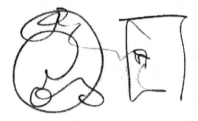

Every so often a fat architect came out of
a green door

It was already spring and the manna came down from the sky as in that famous painting (little people standing in the air) by Magritte. The electric pear burned out, but another pear, large and white, stood in the window.

[14]

I dream that the manuscript has been lost. We (my wife Nurit and I) are looking around and not finding it.

The light bulbs don't go on, and in the other rooms people are sleeping. Who are these people?

And what will happen now to the characters in the manuscript? Some (those who really were) are buried beneath the ground. But where will the others go?

And there are, too, the characters who haven't yet come into the story; and also those who haven't yet been imagined. And who am *I* in this darkness?

I want (precisely because of this uncertainty) to introduce here the Roman emperor Nero. Did they have underwear in those days?

The balcony he sat on while Rome burned was (I know) a Bauhaus balcony like those in Tel Aviv. His mother shouted to him from within the room, but he closed the sliding doors and lowered (how? from outside?) the shutters. Outside (which is to say, in the street) horses and donkeys were fleeing the fire.

Most likely he sang the choral part from Beethoven's *Ninth*, and his testicles (on which there were lice) were squashed against the seat of the chair.

In 1960, we were married, my first wife, Yolanda, and I, at the offices of the rabbinate in Ramat Gan. My father kept to the side, but Ursula, my stepmother, stood like a Japanese wrestler in the middle of the circle.

At 29 Rabbi Kook Street all sorts of German émigrés (on the one hand) and émigrés from Romania and Poland (on the other) were eating from the cake that Ursula baked, and afterward we traveled (Yolanda and I) to the rest home at Kibbutz Nahsholim.

I remember that storks stood in the fish ponds. Yolanda leaned against the window and said:

Storks. Amazingly, she'd uttered this word on our honeymoon (hers and mine). Most likely she was thinking of children.

[15]

In those days, Van Gogh's picture of boats on the shore hung on everyone's wall. Bus drivers earned more than ministers, and civil servants, literally, kicked the citizens around. The sun was formed from thousands of colorful pieces of cloth at the Lodzia factory.

My father's father, Isaac Emerich, rose to the heavens on invisible stairs and took a seat there at a weightless café. On the earth's surface, his widow, my grandmother Emma, bought herself a new coat.

The socialist party held sway in the offices. All sorts of Yiddish speakers spoke to one another so that the others wouldn't understand.

Over all this, snow fell in the mountains and rain on the coastal plain. People had a psychology. Some were battling the subconscious and some the super ego as they crossed the thresholds of their homes and stepped into the street.

The years were turned upside down in their heaviness and, in the passage from one to another, sometimes babies were born.

These small people came from within the women like midgets exiting a tunnel. God himself couldn't have performed a more wondrous act.

If order were introduced into the world one would need to begin on high with the heavens and descend. But if one started from the bottom one would have to start from the sex's opening, which is to say, from my mother, Margaritta.

People say I was born, but they don't enunciate the "n" as they should. One has to fold in the lips with a death-like movement.

[16]

There was a story about a boiler. Yolanda's father, Isaiah, took it up or brought it down. I don't recall.

In any event, we picked up and went to live in Safed, as I held on my lap (in the container of a moving van) an aquarium with three goldfish.

In Safed two madmen were arguing (Itzikl had planes and Yosef Yankele submarines) over who was beating whom. In the end Yosef Yankele vanished (I assume he died and was buried) and Itzikl wandered in the valley and rumor has it that he was devoured by wolves.

There was a very fat man of Romanian extraction (was he called Milu?) who sold pork chops.

The Labor Union's rest home (Beit Bussel) revolved (with that motion of the earth) a bit differently from the city hall across the street. The Yitzhak Luria synagogues, those of the holy Ari (Sephardic and Ashkenazi), were closer to the sun than the home of Schmeel, who sold antiques.

Andreas my father came to visit in Safed but as he walked from the bus station, along a path, a large horse stood in his way. My father showed it the back of his hand and said something like *geh* or *geh weg* but the horse looked at him and didn't move.

If not for a fear of all things surreal, I'd say that my father and the horse were still standing there.

In Safed two madmen were arguing

[17]

I say thank you to the dear souls who have bound themselves to my life and send them forth from literature into the deep regions of the heart that it—art—cannot enter.

If I were able (by means of a deeper covenant than that which exists between author and reader) to fall on people's necks and say to them *Come, let's sit while the tea is steeping, then drink, and you'll tell me about your lives and I will tell of mine,* I'd toss this manuscript into the trash and do precisely that. In such a world the law would forbid the making of fiction.

Therefore, my first wife Varda and my children Yasmin and Tomer and Yotam, and my wife Nurit, will remain outside the realm of this book.

Life is a sacred gift and literature a profane one. If my first wife had brought a catfish up on her hook, and the catfish had crawled across the ground and gotten under her dress, then the catfish and the dress would be here now. But not the woman within the dress. I won't condemn her to a life on paper.

"When Yasmin, my eldest daughter, was born, on the second of January, in Safed, snowflakes were falling from the sky. I stood at the entrance to the hospital hugging the tiny body...." Etcetera. These memories are forbidden here.

As in the drugstore where milkshakes are sold, the memories mingle and, like strawberries, the imagination sweetens the milk: The hospital will be the hospital. And the little girl will come into the world. But at the hospital I'll lie, sick with jaundice, and the little girl, whose name will be Sivan, will be born in a taxi, between the airport at Lod and the Mesubim Junction.

[18]

—*Ani yoledet* (I'm giving birth), Yolanda said.

—*Yoredet?* (Getting out?), the taxi driver said. You can't get out here. There's no place to stop.

—*Ani yoLedet*, Yolanda repeated, emphasizing the "l".

The taxi driver turned off the radio and asked: What?

—*Ani yoledet*, Yolanda said.
—When? asked the driver.
—Now, said Yolanda.

The driver stopped by the side of the road and fled, and so, as a truck driver named Azoulay pulled at her legs, in the Hebrew month of Sivan (June), my daughter Sivan was born.

At the hospital in Safed, Dr. Abramson came (his grandfather's father had disembarked mistakenly at Cork, Ireland, because he'd thought he'd reached America) and stood by my bed.

You have a baby girl, he said.

No I don't, I said.

Yes you do, said Dr. Abramson. I just got a phone call.

From who? I asked.

Someone named Azoulay, Abramson said.

[19]

At the grocery store on Jerusalem Street (in Safed) Hirsch and his wife stood behind the counter and behind their backs were cans of peas and compote and all sorts of noodles.

Above their heads were the discs of light that hover over saints because they said things such as "five liras" or "yellow cheese," which rose directly to heaven.

At noon they closed the store with an iron bar and a padlock then went up to the second floor, which was closer to heaven, to have some soup. At four, Mr. Hirsch and his wife unfastened the lock and took down the iron bar.

At six in the evening Mr. Hirsch turned on the fluorescent light and you could see (until seven) two parallel strips of light along with two haloes.

In front of Mr. Hirsch's store there lay a Mexican dog (that is, a hairless dog) that spoke every so often to invisible dogs. It said: Good. What I've said before I'll say again. You and you and you and you—no. You—yes.

In those days we had no aftershave or deodorant. Only Mr. Reuveni, who was (during the time of the British) a senior clerk, got things like that in the mail from London or Paris.

[20]

In the painters' places the painters painted something that already existed. Some set large canvases up in alleys or in places from which one can see the valley. If they saw a person—they painted a person. If they saw a mountain—they painted a mountain.

There were people there named Zalman Schneur and even one whose name was Arinamal, and the Shekhinah stood half-way up the sky like a large albatross.

Sometimes a person came out of the alley and said *tsafra tava* (good morning, in Aramaic) or *rahmana litzlan* (heaven forfend, in Aramaic) or spit on the sidewalk and spittle sprayed through the air like those diamonds that are passed from hand to hand in Brussels as the merchants say *mazal uverakha* (good luck and a blessing) to close the deal. There were cellars everywhere, and cellars to cellars, in which you could see old chairs (among them that of Elijah), pots, and so forth.

I remember that Srurr, who had a shoe store,

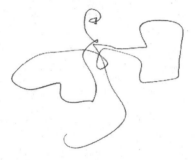

*the Shekhinah stood half-way up the sky like a
large albatross*

came out of his house and didn't return because the colors on his body were erased (as though by divine white-out) one by one from the bottom up.

A woman named Shifra was (by profession) a Lilith. She came out at night from the Ohanas' house or the Farjuns' with her face covered with white makeup and trapped (with her eyes) regions of space.

All stood under the sign of appetite because the number of legs was double that of the number of people.

[21]

Brakha Scheinfeld (who'd come to Safed from New York) came out of the fish store in the Jewish part of town and said, "The Messiah has come." She stuck her hands out before her then sent them to the sides like two ships departing from a port in different directions.

At the end of the stairs that lead from Jerusalem Street to the Painters' Quarter, by the religious school for girls, the postal clerk Rahamim Kadosh stopped me. "Yo-ehlll," he said, "I haven't seen you for ages, nor have you seen me."

Things like this took place approximately twice a week.

In the house at the end of the path, Yolanda washed cloth diapers and hung them up on the roof to dry like flags of surrender. A man named Elimelekh carried the garbage out on the back of a donkey.

Although I have been in the world, I sought (like the philosophers) alternative worlds. The ears stood, for the most part, at the side of my head and whenever I decided to move my hand, my hand moved. Involuntary elements in my body (such as the pancreas) functioned properly.

I planted five carob trees and bougainvillea bushes (which didn't survive the January cold).

I heard a noise in the distance. Most likely the voices of the primordial heavenly bodies growing ever more distant. (A dull sound like Nathan Axelrod. Nathan Alexrod. Nathan Axelrod....)

[22]

Andreas my father and my stepmother Ursula
came to Safed by bus and sat (as in an ancient
Chinese poem) on the balcony. The rays of light
that struck the baby Sivan returned from her
and struck the ends of the nerves in their eyes. I
remember that someone (maybe my stepmother
Ursula) said that very day the German word
schmutzig.

Felitzia, Yolanda's aunt, came to Safed (with
her husband Nahman) and brought a large jar of
plum preserves.

Aunt Felitzia missed some syllables (she said, for
instance, *ee* instead of *he* and *fed* instead of *Safed*).
But sometimes (maybe in order to make up for
what was missing) she'd suddenly utter a word
that bore no relation to what she was saying.

Her husband Nahman was, ironically, a
surveyor. From time to time Felitzia would say:
"Hman, isn't that right?" And Nahman would
answer: "Yes, yes it is."

The dead too (whose names were Sha'ul) came to

visit, and as it is with them (with the dead) they had trouble holding onto their tea cups.

The world (they complained) is too material. As, for example, in the parable of Plato's cave (they said), in fact *they*—the dead—are more real. Especially, so they said, if one takes into account the length of time (from their death and on).

Actually it's the little things that make people happy. Like, for instance, the fact that in German one says *Schnurrbart* (that is, a string-beard, or mustache) or that, very close to the ground, there are violet flowers one can barely see in the spring beneath the scotch grass.

[23]

Here we'd do well to count the various sorts of birds:

There's the bird that clasps wall-clocks under its wings. And next (in descending order) the phoenix. And then there's the sympathetic bird. The sycamore bird (which tends sycamores). The frozen bird. The bird of the right. The birds of the belt (the waists of which are extremely narrow).

The hygiene bird and all sorts of migratory birds.

Time after time Yolanda escaped to her parents (Isaiah and Esther), who lived at 7 Ahuzat Bayit Street in Tel Aviv.

She was always right because by nature a woman is better constructed. She's music and she's the musician, and the man is little more than the person who stands at the musician's side and turns the pages.

Her body is better constructed as well. When she walks (even when she's ugly) her strides are aligned with the buried scales (like that magnetic pole) in the belly of the earth.

From Tel Aviv Yolanda sent me postcards containing only questions, such as: Have you thought of this? Or: What will be? Or: Don't you think the time has come?

The heart follows the heart. I remember a man who, on the way to the office, along the main road, fell to his knees.

[24]

In the end Yolanda came back to Safed but if you looked carefully you could see that her lips were pursed.

Sometimes a window broke or a bowl shattered like the sound of cymbals or castanets in the symphony orchestra.

In those days we also became acquainted (Yolanda and I) with people named Shmosh-kovitz.

Mr. Shmoshkovitz and his wife veered to the side as they walked. That is, because of the way their legs were built, or for another reason unbeknownst to us, they'd walk along diagonal lines.

Therefore, when they had to get from one place to another they'd walk farther than other people (to the side and back, to the side and back, etcetera).

In addition, covered by a yellow cloth, a large organ stood in their house.

"One day we'll play the organ," Mr. Shmoshkovitz said (even on the couch he'd veer to the side). Mrs. Shmoshkovitz confirmed her husband's statement from the other couch as she inverted the sentence and led with the subject: "The organ we will play."

But one day movers came and took the organ out of the house, its large pipes pointing, like katyusha rockets, toward Ein Zeitim.

Mr. Shmoshkovitz and his wife continued veering to the side as they walked (that is, from one side of the sidewalk to the other side of the sidewalk), slowly advancing, twice a week, toward Jerusalem Street.

"The Catholics," Mr. Shmoshkovitz said, "bought the organ," and his wife added, "in Tiberias."

[25]

And there were also the lunatics who drove large buses from place to place. And the madmen who worked in the Interior Ministry, and those who slaughtered chickens (they were called

Shteinmetz), and the mad silversmiths who sat in little shops etcetera.

Mad winds blew in the fall and therefore large fish came out of the mouth of the Jordan River and walked by foot all the way to Safed along a winding road, past Rosh Pina, and sat at the corner café beneath the pictures of Elvis Presley.

And sometimes you'd hear a man screaming Shimon or Pinhas most likely because Shimon or Pinhas had gone away and he could find no peace until he could see him again.

Wedding ceremonies were conducted at Hotel Herzliya or the Central Hotel.

Usually the grooms were skinny and the family members sat at tables with their skulls cleft (as though by an ax). Children ran about (as in Breughel's well-known painting) beneath the tables, in a process of giving and taking.

Girls from the religious school Hokhmat Ya'akov put plates filled with sandwiches and also a pickle onto the large speakers and a short man from Alma or Dalton sang wedding songs.

Most of the brides were named Miriam, and you could see them get into the taxi (after the

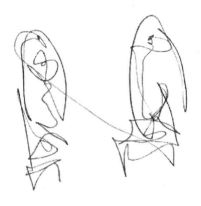

large fish . . . sat at the corner café

wedding) as they gathered up the white dress and, for a moment, exposed a thigh.

[26]

In those days I read a book by a philosopher named Rudolf Carnap. It was written there that Rudolf Carnap believed only in the senses (that is, in patches of color, and so on).

In addition Rudolf Carnap believed in logic because logic (so he said) doesn't depend on patches of color. It is true (so he said) in any event.

Mr. Katzover, who was the honorary French Consul under the Turks, was also familiar with Rudolf Carnap's theories, though he'd heard of them only indirectly.

Because I'd read that book, I saw large patches of color. For example, the Lower Galilee.

Synagogues and stray dogs confirmed Rudolf Carnap's theory. For (as I saw it) even if we peel back from the old doors the various layers of paint, there will appear, in any event, other colors.

The sky too (that is, the great blue surface) confirms Carnap's claims.

I also read a book by Moritz Schlick, who was Rudolf Carnap's friend, but he said similar things.

Sometimes (during the sixties) the earth spun too quickly and therefore the sun rose and set swiftly. In roughly an hour. Maybe forty minutes.

[27]

A woman named Mina Katznelson, from Kibbutz Kinneret, sold me five beehives.

I put the hives in five wooden boxes and placed the boxes in an open field near the village of Gush Halav.

The bees, which clearly had heard of onomatopoeia, buzzed ceaselessly. Sometimes they gathered near the entrance to the box like Jews in front of a synagogue on the high holy days.

Some of them found (by means of color, thus confirming Carnap's theory) distant fields of wildflowers, and they returned to the box and called the others toward those fields.

The heart can't bear these words ("distant fields").

Stairwells make us weep. And small kitchens. Sometime you see a fork and you just want to die.

There is no limit to the beauty of things. Stooped people. Trees. All sorts of things in the courtyard (an old motorbike, for instance).

I remember a man crossing the waiting room at the train station.

[28]

In 1966 Moshe Kroi consumed some seven containers of buttermilk in Jerusalem. At dinner (in the apartment we'd rented in Bayit vaGan) he wrote on the table the entirety of Spinoza's teaching in logical signs. Tzvi Daliyot, a lecturer in logic, sat on the other side of the table and looked at Yolanda.

The little girl Sivan was there, and also Yoel Hoffmann, who eludes me continuously and whose nature it is hard to grasp.

At nine, roughly, the neighbor from the adjacent apartment—her name was Nitza—came to the table and her breasts rose over the logical signs.

From those same days I recall the old kettle and the word *shokh* (dying off), which someone uttered (as in "the *shokh* of the storm").

A Swedish man I once knew in Amsterdam came to visit and brought with him an empty suitcase containing only a large doll. A distant cousin, an engineer, came to show us the new Contessa (the car) he'd just purchased.

Everything that happened then was completely logical, but Yolanda gave birth to her baby too early and he lay there in a glass box for three or four months.

[29]

The university was divided (like Jerusalem itself) between the disciples of Bar-Hillel and those of Natan Rotenstreich. The disciples of Bar-Hillel said things that were true but utterly worthless while Rotenstreich's disciples talked utter nonsense that filled the heart with joy.

At Givat Ram there were lecturers who, on the way to the cafeteria, would suddenly leap into the air. Some of them walked with a slouch by bushes along the path.

In large halls shaped like stadiums, hundreds of people sat and listened to lectures on sociology.

The baby lying in the glass box was so very dear to my heart that I wanted to call it (in order to fend off the pain) Chedorlaomer.

I remember that I walked alone to two synagogues (one Sephardic and the other Ashkenazi) and prayed to God that he might leave the glass box.

Other Jews looked at me and didn't understand, but the prayer-books they shouted contained just the right synthesis between the teachings of Bar-Hillel and those of Rotenstreich.

[30]

A Japanese monk came to Ein Kerem and we sat with him for a week, like frogs.

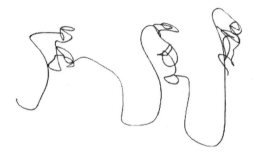

there were lecturers who, on the way to the cafeteria, would suddenly leap into the air

On the third day a woman wept heavily and on the sixth day a man laughed. You could hear the stone cutters, and the sound of the wind in the pines.

He asked about the sound of one hand but most likely was thinking of his elderly mother in Toyohashi.

How many hairs did he have on his head? Where is he now?

On the bus from Ein Kerem to Bayit vaGan we underwent a transformation. Suddenly we saw the dusty windshield and the stone homes along the highway. We knew that it was June.

We brought dogs into the home. The light stood up straight and the surface of the earth stretched out before us. The telephone book became a kind of literature.

But the baby that came home (we'll call him Mikha'el) doubled life, as babies do. He was mine. A mortal. God of Israel.

[31]

Andreas my father and Ursula, my stepmother, came to see the baby and sat on the balcony (this time in Bayit vaGan). You could see the university from there and my father asked where the relevant department was.

Neighbors (like Mrs. Tannenbaum) came to look at the baby and also (I recall) our neighbor Nitza, who bent over the carriage and you could see her breasts.

Moshe Kroi, who was at the time writing his essay on egoism, held the baby in his arms and squeezed him toward his body, like a pirate who'd dug and discovered a treasure. Even King Hussein fired (in 1967) several rounds from the cannons.

Mrs. Piatelli taught me Japanese twice a week from an old book and the heavy scent of thirty cats hung in the air.

Daughter—*musume*
Baby—*akatchan*
Morning—*asa*

Night—*yoru*
I (if you're a man)—*boku*
I (if you're a woman)—*watakushi*
Thank you—*arigato*

[32]

The setting of this book (I neglected to mention) is the world. Bugs are in it. Nor is history ignored. Agamemnon, for instance. Textile stores—in their places—come into it. On Paris Square, for instance. In Haifa.

And countless envoys (with pizza, and so forth). Some ride bikes.

Although it's nearly flat, the dimensions of space in the book are infinite. It's impossible to mention all the stars, but they too enter into its equation.

The lecturer in logic, Tzvi Daliyot, broke his right leg and therefore someone else (maybe Poznanski) tested us on Tarski's book.

But as in the old English song, a certain woman cooked some porridge and the porridge boiled up over the pot and spilled out of the kitchen windows (of the cafeteria) and covered the lecture halls and the National Library up to the height of its entrance doors.

Most of the exams were cancelled, but because the municipal snow-plows removed some of the porridge, students from the philosophy department showed up.

The scent of porridge and sugar hung in the air, and so it was hard to concentrate on Tarski's argument.

The entire second exam period was, as a result, a mess. But, to our great amazement, outside, where the buses departed for the nearby suburbs, an old Arab stood and said to each one of us, *salaam aleikum*.

[33]

Sometimes Yolanda grew silent because she was angry or hurt and we (like kings we hide behind the plural) sought for ourselves the mother of the son of God, whose mercies are infinite.

We said to ourselves that a woman would save us. After all, even she-wolves had nursed newborn human beings.

We were so very lonely beneath the heavens that we wanted to hug ourselves, but couldn't find any free arms.

We could have been redeemed when we bought grapefruit juice, but we weren't. We could have been redeemed when we sat beside a person on the bus, but we weren't.

There were so many of us in a single body and it too was hidden by clothes.

Once we asked a foreign woman on Jaffa Road: Do you love me?

Mrs. Piatelli was a widow because someone had shot her husband next to the Cinema North box-office, in Tel Aviv.

Mrs. Piatelli went to the prison and forgave the murderer. She kept some thirty cats well fed and taught music and odd Japanese.

Later (in the order of things) Mrs. Piatelli travelled to Germany and jumped off a bridge (I

There were so many of us in a single body

don't recall the name of the town) into one of those great rivers.

More or less around the same time, two women from the Association of Soldiers' Mothers crossed the Jordan and one of them drowned.

In what is now being said there is not a shred of humor. It doesn't have anything to do with literature: Mrs. Piatelli and the woman from the Association (her name, unfortunately, escapes me) were devoured by fish.

[34]

At night we slept (we and Yolanda) back to back while each one saw, as though in a bubble emerging from the head of a comic-strip character, different dreams.

Yolanda most likely dreamed of great gardens. Clay pots. Dalmatians.

We (which is to say, I) saw heavier dreams. Landslides in the mountains and an entire town with its golden church spires buried beneath the dirt. Men spreading newspapers out on the floor and reading things in them that make the heart tremble.

It's all so self-evident why Joyce wrote, for some twenty years, a book without any real words in it. After all, one could die from the clear-cut borders between one word and another: Pot. Skyscraper. File. Scandal. Dentures. Scabies. Snow. Old age. Flute. Cobalt. Socialism.

Sometimes we made instant coffee with three teaspoons of sugar (as Yolanda liked it) and put it before her.

[35]

We went to the Japanese monk (next to Augusta Victoria Hospital) and spoke with him about space and time. *Time does not exist,* he said, waving a hand that bore a watch.

Our lives come from no-where. We were born and not born. Because of this, everything (nothing) is so very clear.

An insurance agent came to us and his socks had fallen. He'd lost the elastic band that held the socks against his leg and we understood (his name was Minkovski) that these socks were located at the center of the universe and all distances to and from them were equal.

Then at least (Minkovski says) insure the apartment. But the apartment is rented. And therefore he walks, his back toward us, toward the door and goes into the street.

I remember, too, Mr. Har Zahav (once Goldberg), who wore a suit even during heat waves.

[36]

The cousin who'd bought the Contessa came again and spread the family tree out on a table. It turns out that my grandfather's father was a cooper and a cavalryman in the Austro-Hungarian army. His wife played first violin in the Bratislava Symphony.

He (that is, the cousin) observed baby Mikha'el with an engineer's expertise.

An insurance agent came to us and his
socks had fallen

We too (that is, I) are exceedingly funny in the eyes of others. The way we walk resembles more the dragging of legs along as the body pitches forward. The ears are rather large because they hear only some of the sounds that exist. Entire monologues are lost (especially the voices of men).

In the end we're a praying mantis inclined to melancholy, and it's hard in the extreme to believe that in our next life we'll become a cheerful washerwoman.

Also the way we sleep at night closely resembles the praying posture of the mantis.

Naked and penniless we could have sold ourselves perhaps for seventy lira (in the currency of the time) especially because we'd mastered Kant and Spinoza. We have no idea at all about the subconscious (which most likely isn't worth much).

Illnesses: Diabetis Renalis. A percent or two of sugar in the urine.

[37]

And the heart as well. The heart inclines (as in

In the end we're a praying mantis inclined to melancholy

a mechanical dysfunction) inward. It sees in particular its own sorrow, like that boy on the Christians' holiday who hides inside a pumpkin shell and asks for candy.

Maybe (on account of the egocentricity) only fifty lira. And in fact we haven't read Spinoza, or Kant (only a page here and there). We're allergic to Sigmund Freud and to Darwin (who made his wife play chess with him every evening) and to Karl Marx. Also to certain politicians on the Left.

We like Moroccans and Russians and yogurt with berries and (on television) Benny Hill.

My wife says: For some reason, flaws seem like virtues when you talk about them. Why don't you write that you're as sensitive as a mimosa (that plant that closes when you touch it)? Or that you're so easily insulted?

(In our favor: We drive the sun.)

[38]

In 1970 the Japanese gave us a stipend to study their philosophy *there*.

At the airport, in the city of Osaka, the baby Mikha'el (who was by then already four) saw what he saw and walked along on his own into the huge crowd and vanished.

Half an hour later we found him, his one hand in the hand of a Persian man and the other hand holding a large bar of chocolate.

The Persian man explained that the boy had grabbed on to his hand and led him to the candy stand, all the while intently looking for chocolate, which later turned out (so Mikha'el explained) to be filled with cherry cream.

At the entrance to the hotel, two women wearing Japanese clothes pointed to our feet and screamed, with great alarm, *kutsu!*

Since Mrs. Piatelli had taught us only obscure grammatical structures we didn't know that *kutsu* meant shoes.

We took off our shoes at the hotel entrance and walked across the straw floor, as the child Sivan (who now was eight) and the boy Mikha'el leapt (with joy) into the air.

[39]

In the morning we received rice and dried fish with seaweed in wooden bowls, and the children burst out in tears when it became clear that there was nothing else to eat.

From that morning I recall the dog I saw in the back alley, perhaps because he saw me *as well*.

I remember too that I drank (later on I'll return to the first-person plural) a very sweet drink from small bottles.

I didn't know the value of money then (the drink was very expensive) and I gulped down six bottles, one after the other. Only several weeks later did I learn that this drink was intended to increase one's sexual potency, and that, at most, one should consume just a bottle a week.

At noon a man came and greeted us. He bowed deeply and gave a long speech in Japanese. Each sentence began with *warewarewa*, and this too I couldn't recall from Mrs. Piatelli's lessons.

I imagine that he said (more or less) that *warewarewa* great joy that we've come. That *warewarewa* hope that our honorable stay in the land

He bowed deeply and gave a long speech in Japanese

of the rising sun will be very pleasant, and that *warewarewa* have complete confidence that we'll find our studies very helpful.

Two days later, at a festive ceremony (full of *warewarewas*) the school for the study of the Japanese language opened and there we learned that the meaning of this word was, when spoken by men, "we" (which is to say, them).

[40]

We (which is to say, I) studied for six months and lived with Mr. Sakamoto and his American wife, Nancy.

At that time (in the month of November) Mishima Yukio committed suicide and Mr. Sakamoto spent the night in the room of the young Japanese woman who lived in the court-yard (in any event, Nancy was some forty centi-meters taller than him).

Jay, the Yogi (a Jew from the Bronx), lived there too, and he recommended that everyone drink their own urine. And Dan and Mary, who'd come from Connecticut, lived there, and also an

Indonesian who each day prepared a dish made of bananas and pork fat.

The child Mikha'el contracted mumps and so for three full days he kept a large cardboard box beneath the sheets.

There was only a single bathtub there, made of wood, and so we bathed together, in pairs, at appointed times, just once a week. I remember that the child Sivan behaved toward us (which is to say, to me) as though the image of her stark naked father was an everyday sight.

Next to Mr. Sakamoto's house was a large park with a temple, and each morning a pregnant woman emerged from the fog.

[41]

It's hard to bear books. A man sees a tree and writes *I saw a tree*. And there are books about books.

Once I met an old woman in a corridor of Beilinson Hospital. She pointed to her feet and asked (perhaps five times), *What for?*

Sometimes it seems that the world is full of unnecessary things. People named Rudolf. All sorts of sketches. Entire buildings. You walk along in the street and in the display window (behind glass) you see pastrami. Dictionaries (with words in them like *Schorenstein*). A car beeping as it travels in reverse. Signs.

Imagine for a moment a Jew and the Jew is sitting on a chair and the chair is in the world. The great loneliness of the Jew. How much space does a man with a chair require, and how much is he given.

[42]

At a considerable distance from there (that is, from Osaka), in Ramat Gan, my Aunt Edith fell and broke the glass in the door between the bedroom and the balcony. The glazier (so she wrote) couldn't find the right glass in the matte yellow tint and therefore had to settle for orange. Aunt Olga (so she wrote), Ladislaus's wife, insulted her. Is it right (she asked) that the Japanese word for thank you so closely resembles the Latin word for alligator?

How much space does a man with a chair require

Every day we wrote down in the big notebook, at least a hundred times, five Chinese characters. Woman = a picture of a person bent over. Man = a rice paddy and, at the bottom, a clenched hand. One = a single line. Two = two lines. Three = three lines. A married woman = a person bent over (that is, a woman) and a broom.

We went to Arashiyama, a place where cormorants dive and bring up fish from the river. All around, in fiery colors, maple trees stood, but the heart (which is called *kokoro* in Japanese) saw other dreams.

[43]

A woman who says the word *butterfly* (I've forgotten in which context) and later, at a hotel covered with red wall prints, confesses, completely naked, that she belongs to an ostracized sect.

A woman whose face is covered with white powder and whose feet, which touch the wooden counter of the bar, are bare.

A woman-mother, like a Buddhist Madonna with an infant (which is us) in her lap.

A woman standing at a street corner and saying quietly: *Anata?* (You?) *Watashi?* (Me?) *OK?*

The fragrance of a strange perfume in the bookstore.

[44]

We must confess before the reader (if there is a reader) that we and he are alike.

We eat a hot meal and he, too, eats a hot meal. We look in the shop window (at electrical appliances) and he, too, looks in the shop window (at electrical appliances). We come home and he comes home as well. At night we turn over in our sleep, and at night he turns over in his sleep. We lie, and he lies too.

Once I saw a reader who lied to a bus driver. And a reader who shouted. I saw readers running swiftly at a demonstration (or disturbance). Readers whose shoe-size was large (forty six and higher).

And a reader whose name was Nebentzal. A very skinny man. He gets up and walks from the desk to the bookcase and back. And his wife is in the kitchen. This is the reader Nebentzal and that is his wife.

[45]

At the closing ceremony of the language school large fans hung over our heads. And each one had four wings, as in the prophetic vision.

The East German gave a speech in Japanese on behalf of us all, and he used, as he should, the word *ishokenmei*, which means "to make every possible effort with all the powers we have at our disposal."

It was already April and the cherry trees were in blossom, and we (which is to say, Yolanda and I and the two children) picked ourselves up and moved from Osaka to Kyoto.

I'm reminded of Niels Holgersen and his journeys on the back of a wild goose. How the fields looked from high in the sky. Like a painting by

This is the reader Nebentzal

Kandinsky. And tiny houses. All of humanity spread before him.

But he didn't see them eating bread. Or fixing an old chair in the attic. He heard only the language of the geese, which had just two words. One that was more or less equivalent to what we call "the sky" and the other for everything else.

Once, in New Haven, England, I saw a sick seagull. It climbed up onto a pipe sticking out of the ground and looked into a toy-store window.

[46]

Professor Take'utchi greeted us in his room at Kyoto University.

He spoke about Bishop Berkeley. The world (he said) according to Bishop Berkeley consists entirely of pictures. And the pictures are in the head. And the head too—is a picture.

We drank (the professor and I) green tea and ate a seaweed pastry. And then Professor Take'utchi spoke of Hegel.

We thought about Hegel's death. At that time

there were certainly pajamas with embroidered lacework collars. And physicians scrambled from room to room, holding in their hands large bottles of urine.

At approximately six, an assistant by the name of Nakamura entered the room. He bowed deeply and led us to a restaurant that specialized in noodles (which are called, in Japanese, *udon*).

We sat (the three of us) on the straw floor and, with wooden chopsticks, brought the noodles up from the soup bowl. Hot vapor enveloped us and, for a few moments, we lost one another.

[47]

In the place where we lived, with Mrs. Ishihara, there was a mound of stones. According to Mrs. Ishihara, the gods who watched over the house dwelled there.

Mrs. Ishihara's daughter, who had a wooden leg, limped to church on Sunday, and once a year, on Souls' Day, a Buddhist priest came to Mrs. Ishihara's house and prayed to the family ancestors before a box in which photographs of the dead had been placed.

Before he came to Kyoto, Mrs. Ishihara's father (so she told us) had met a demon in the mountains and talked with it throughout the night. The demon also spoke in a village dialect, although it had a different form. Something like a man. But not a man.

What did they talk about? This the father didn't say, but ever since that night a kind of furrow appeared on his forehead, like those cracks that appear in the ground after an earthquake.

That same year autumn came early and by October the cold winds were already blowing. Letters (including some that hadn't yet been read) flew about in the air.

[48]

Dogs came to visit us. There was one that was mangy and went up to the heap of stones where the Shinto gods were dwelling. And one that was missing a leg. And the black hairy one.

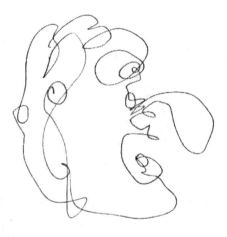

The demon also spoke in a village dialect

We could see that they possessed (despite what some philosophers think) a deep consciousness. The id in particular. The superego was less developed, and therefore their personalities were revealed.

The mangy one (very likely called Abramov) had a fatalistic streak. He had already seen the dark side of life and therefore his mind was at rest. Or he rested his mind, if you place the predicate first.

The dog with the missing leg clearly had little in the way of appetite. He kept only the larger account like a precocious boy who has trouble with math. Something like the philosopher Parmenides: "What-is is and what-isn't isn't."

The hairy black dog revealed his heart with ease. Pain = pain. Joy = joy. And so on. Some of the Rishis in the Himalayas reached his spiritual level, perhaps, but couldn't match him in other respects.

There were also opinionated crows, like teachers at a theological seminary, and a bird no one saw and whose name is hard to find in dictionaries.

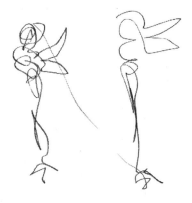

There were also opinionated crows, like teachers at
a theological seminary

[49]

Every morning Mrs. Kido came back home from
her night job in the Gion quarter, with a cloud of
sake before her like the pillar (of fire) that went
before the camp.

"*Ohayo gozaimas*" (good morning) she would
say, and her voice sounded like glass cups.

Sometimes we dreamed that we were changing our
lives. Instead of going to the bus stop and then to
the university, we're walking with Mrs. Kido into
her home. She leaves the *obi* in the foyer and takes
off the *kimono* in the hall outside the bedroom.

We (which is to say, I) pour out a large glass of
Kirin beer and turn on the television to the sumo
channel.

When she wakes up (at dusk), Mrs. Kido says
anata (you) gently and we say only *mm* ... (as in
confirming one's presence in a roll call) and so
on year after year, until we die open-mouthed in
front of the television and the old geisha brings
our ashes home in a vase.

[50]

In the meantime the girl Sivan goes to a Japanese
school and Mikha'el the boy goes to kindergarten,
where a teacher named Kontani points out things
and teaches him their names (chair = *isu*, window
= *mado*, etcetera).

She points to herself as well (she touches, as
the Japanese do, her nose) and says *Kontani sensei*
(the teacher Kontani). The boy Mikha'el comes
home and teaches *us* Japanese: *isu* = chair, *mado* =
window. *Kontani sensei* = nose.

The girl Sivan speaks Japanese fluently but while
all the children draw the rock garden at the Ryoanji
temple with complete accuracy, she makes some
rocks bigger and others smaller and adds rocks of
her own. The art teacher (who most likely has not
heard of impressionism) calls on her to "respect
reality."

We (that is, I) respect reality deeply. When a
woman comes—we see a woman. When a Korean
comes—we see a Korean. And beyond this,

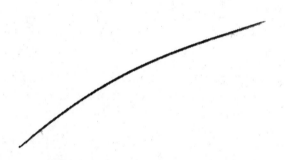

We (that is, I) respect reality deeply

we stretch out a sky just as the creator of all the
worlds did.

[51]

We've already mentioned that we drive the sun
daily from East to West so that it sets (just as John
the Baptist drove the heads of believers) into the
sea.

Then we bring up the moon and hold it high
all night until the arm grows tired.

We do all this while the reader is sleeping in bed,
and also write (with the other hand) a dimestore
novel in Yiddish. About a good-for-nothing
man, a one-eyed, fat, and smelly merchant from
Warsaw, who violated the innocence of virgins.

Our hearts go out to the virgins (among them
several red-heads) and we want to comfort them
for their bitter fate and do so with our free hand or
put the moon down where we like and hug them
with both hands.

We are in Kyoto and long for Kyoto. We long for a
foot (ours or another's). For toes. Weeds (especially

those that grow in the walls of government office-buildings) drive us mad.

[52]

We're reading Buddhist texts with master Hirano. The sound of one hand (he says) when there is nothing to strike. Everything strikes itself. If you see a flower—you don't think of eyes. If you hear a sound—you don't think of ears.

It's like a man who comes to Kiev and at the train station has his wallet stolen. Now he's in Kiev and has no wallet. He wants to call the police, but there is no phone.

Master Hirano compares various versions of ancient texts and at eight o'clock, exactly, he pops the top off a bottle of Sapporo and watches the series about a detective, McCloud, who comes from Texas and joins the New York City Police Department.

Sometimes the earth quakes and the heavy beams at the wooden temple creak.

[53]

Professor Take'utchi's mother dies and we console him with the traditional Hebrew expression, "May you know no more sorrow." It's extremely difficult to translate these words into Japanese, and Professor Take'utchi grows alarmed.

In the hall he walks very close to the wall, stooped over, as though he were carrying his dead mother. Nakamura the assistant walks behind him. The halls at Kyoto University are quite dark, but in the end they (that is, Professor Take'utchi and his assistant, Nakamura) exit into the street.

Fog covers the city of Kyoto entirely, and the booksellers take their wares from the sidewalk into the stores, since the pedestrians walk by as though they were blind and knock over the books of philosophy, economics, and history.

We (which is to say, I) walk through this fog to the Gion quarter and look for whorehouses, but the steps lead toward a wine cellar, or basement, and in any case the hour is late and the streetlights stand inside the fog like candles burning for the dead.

[54]

A man named Maximov comes to visit us. He's a technician for industrial looms and has been sent by the Haifa factory to Osaka to install computers.

With him comes Or Hayyim, the technician he's replacing (that is, Or Hayyim is returning to Israel), and the two of them sit on Mrs. Ishihara's wooden floor and talk about textiles.

A marvelous symmetry could be discerned in Or Hayyim. Every limb on the right was matched by a limb on the left, and his head too was constructed in a similar fashion.

It's harder to remember Maximov, but most likely he too was symmetrical. Usually they (that is, Maximov and Or Hayyim) agreed with one another. Which is to say, there was an inner symmetry between them.

Behind the window stood Mrs. Ishihara's walnut tree, and you could compare it (that is, the tree) with the textile technicians.

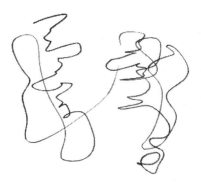

Usually they (that is, Maximov and Or Hayyim)
agreed with one another

[55]

It occurs to us that the German word *nie* (never) is very funny. Such a short word, for eternity. Or the word *und* (and), which so closely resembles *hund* (dog).

And there are names (like Tzippora—Hebrew for a female bird) that break one's heart.

A large, hairy man (perhaps from the Ainu tribe, in northern Japan) is named after the hummingbird.

Now I can reveal a secret. The elementary school at the corner of Herzl Street and Rabbi Kook (which belonged to the General Zionist Party) had wings.

Correct. Usually the wings were folded. But in the morning, when we sang "Adon Olam" (Lord of the World—who reigned etcetera)—it (that is, the school) spread its wings and you could see them from the window.

These are memories of childhood. Just as one recalls a chamber pot or a washboard or broken steps.

In truth, Rachel Green, in first grade, captured my heart, and if she reads this book (now she's sixty eight), she'll know I liked her.

[56]

In 1974 we came home on a plane full of musicians (Sibelius, Shostakovich, etcetera).

Andreas my father, and Ursula, my stepmother, hung a large cardboard sign in the hall (WELCOME), and on the table they set out all sorts of gifts for the children, and a marzipan cake.

Later we went (that is, I went) to the barbershop and the barber asked me about Japan and Korea and told me all sorts of things.

The sky was very blue (it was June) and we saw that behind the Urbach's and the Leikechmann's, they'd built a new house.

There were pigeons in the air and I remembered how Micha Urbach's mother would stand on the balcony, in just her bra, and call him home for dinner.

[57]

The old house in Safed was full of dust but the carob trees had grown.

Our lives (that is, my life) had taken on some three thousand Zen riddles, but these things brought Yolanda no joy. Probably she said to herself that it's better for a person to be without riddles, or to have all of his riddles solved, so as to be free for other things.

We (which is to say, I) wanted one of two things. Either that thoughts would vanish once and for all, as Hiroshima and Nagasaki had vanished, or that there would be just this one thought, that of the infant, in the Christian icons, lying in the Madonna's lap.

In the meantime, a man named Zemelweiss disturbed our peace. We too (which is to say, they), he said, we too are originally from Kronshtadt, which today is called Brashov, and some of us come from Targu Mures. We really should try to find out, he said, who married whom, and then we'll know just how we're related.

[58]

The cousin who bought the Contessa came to Safed and asked to see the oil painting of a family ancestor. But the painting, which had been in the basement for years, had gotten wet from the rain and all that was left of it was the canvas and frame.

In fact one has to seek out the dead by other means. One has to put eye-masks on (in Japanese they're called *mekakushi*) and lie down in the dark.

At first they'll come from Auschwitz because their bodies were burned and their movements are light. They don't need to break through the crust of the earth like the others.

In the end, all will be gathered—and the dead who aren't from the family too, like those who come to strangers' weddings or the funerals of people they never knew.

You're surprised by the power of the dead, in that their certainty (with regard to the future) is absolute. There are no greetings. Nor is there any reproof. There is no noise. No smell. Not even an image.

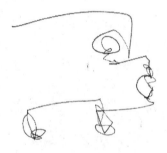

The cousin who bought the Contessa came to Safed

[59]

And now the time has come to say a few words about this beloved land, which we're always leaving and to which we always return.

The eyes don't see everything, but there is a port in the mountain town of Safed and large ships anchor at its pier. You can see the tips of the masts already from the village of Rameh. Some of the old olive trees along the way are Crusaders who froze in place on the fields.

You see a ruin in the Galilee and you understand how miserable the castles in Europe are. The Shekhinah reveals itself like a slice of bread. Everyone plays the flute.

What would we do without the Arabs, God bless them. And without the Romanian immigrants. And without the Moroccans. Is there anywhere else in the world where you fall to the ground, epileptic, and all at once thirty hands reach down your throat to free your tongue?

And we haven't yet spoken of the red sun that

there is a port in the mountain town of Safed

sometimes rises from the opposite direction (which is to say, from the sea).

[60]

I recall that Ursula, my stepmother, said the word *Bluse* (blouse).

Sometimes things take on the shape of the words that signify them. Most blouses do in fact resemble a *Bluse*. Or take a name like Aurelia. A girl whose name is Aurelia looks like Aurelia. It's impossible to call a man "David" whose name is Pinhas, and vice versa.

Sleep, too, is something odd. You go from here to there and suddenly freeze in place. And sneezing, which frightens others greatly.

If, for instance, we go to a bakery and walk in through the front door and cross the large room where the machines shape the dough into the form of the bread and then go out the back door we can see a man asking: Why did you cut through the bakery?

Once we saw a woman of Moldavian extraction. She was studying Hebrew in a language school but used only the word "just."

Or take, for example, the extended family named Buchbinder. In fact not all of them bind books. And there are, remarkably, bookbinders with other names entirely.

Or the pipes that are laid. They're straight until they reach a bend and then they turn in another direction.

The only logical thing in the world is the prayer *Barukh ata adonai* (Blessed art Thou O Lord our God). Not because of its religiosity. But because of its sounds, as each one leads to the one that follows.

[61]

At Passover all sorts of visitors came to Safed. Moshe Kwitner (who in sixth grade we called "Ginger-root") came with his wife and three children. His wife (Shoshana) sat excitedly with Yolanda because they found they had something in common and spoke about it from all sorts of perspectives. Ginger-root took us aside and asked about Japanese whorehouses.

And Yolanda's aunt and uncle came (her father Isaac's sister and her husband), who had a leather factory in Kiryat Motzkin. And Meshullam, with whom we'd served in the army (together with Bertonov), came in a brand-new Ford.

We thought that this was a normal life and, as proof, we bought a poppy-seed cake and made instant coffee for everyone, with milk and two teaspoons of sugar.

[62]

Life, we thought to ourselves, is a matter of back and forth. Give and take. One comes and goes and there is no end to it.

We saw the literary pages in the weekend paper and understood that around their sorrow people construct a story. Some make do with *realia* alone. If someone says, Where's the shirt I wore yesterday, they write: Re'uma, where's the shirt I wore yesterday (and they add, "he said"). Others give us a bit of hope by ending the story with words such as "and in the East the dawn was already breaking."

We run into each other like balls on a billiards table, and the only thing left is the sound of the knocking.

But in fact the Tzederboim family (a father, mother, and five- or six-year old) go for a walk each evening on Jerusalem Street. Every so often they stand and say something to the boy and the boy laughs and raises his hands and his father carries him for a short distance.

[63]

At roughly that time we began to hold forth at the university (of Tel Aviv or Haifa).

The university is built (apart from the cafeteria) on the assumption that there is:

    a) a world;

    b) words that describe it.

And one might also add:

    c) words that describe the words that describe it.

But in fact the Tzederboim family

Within all this, people walk about with names like Kaplinksi or Eshtahaul or Bar-Ziva, and girls walk around in various colors, and all enter and exit rooms with the numbers 526 or 3002.

A man whose name is Bebaleh walks the wrong way in the corridor. Not down it, but across it. From wall to wall.

A thread of sadness is drawn over the face of the university because, like the Madonna, it gives birth to divine children. Within that noise the placental waters flow and the baby comes into the world toward the glass windows and the stone walls, very slowly, within the process of an utterly natural birth. His body fills the bookshelves and lecture halls, like winter fog coming over Reykjavik.

[64]

It's hard to remember precisely the year and month and day when the cow fell on the storage-shed roof in Safed.

The roof, which was made of some artificial

material (asbestos or the like) cracked in half and the cow landed flat on the storage-shed floor between old dolls, philosophy books, and sheet music for the violin.

That reminds me of one of the Church Fathers. Maybe the one (I've forgotten his name) who sailed from Tyre to Alexandria.

At sea, the boat was about to break up and he called loudly to his God. But when he finally set foot on the pier, he walked, wobbling slightly, to the custom officers' chamber and asked them for a drink that was common then (something alcoholic, made from barley).

We're telling all this because the heart is refusing to speak of the sorrow of sleepless nights. When the innermost cows low and try to get out of their sheds. Woe is me. And my wife. And my children.

[65]

A beautiful woman who looked like my witness-on-high played the harp beside the widow Meyuhas's curtain store on Jerusalem Street.

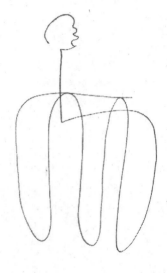

*A beautiful woman who looked like my
witness-on-high*

People put coins in the cardboard box before her and it was clear from her face that she was remembering Pennsylvania, or Vermont, and a house with a vestibule (I've never quite understood the meaning of that word) and fir trees.

We saw ourselves following the harpist from that place and onward in dusty buses, in five-dollar-a-night hotels, from country to country.

A man takes a woman to be his woman and a woman takes a man to be her man and water comes from water and air from air, like once, in a city called Maryport, on the east coast of England, I saw an old house and pier which were, perfectly, what they were.

[66]

A careful reader will, I think, notice (if he looks at a map) that Maryport is on the *west* coast of England. *That*, exactly, is the hidden power. To transport an entire city, with its churches and markets and port (and even the ships that have anchored there) from coast to coast.

Or it's possible (by virtue of that same power) to create a person. For instance, a person whose name is Douglas and to bring him to Yolanda. So the two of them will sit on the balcony, on Purim or the fifteenth of Shevat (Arbor Day), and look out (together) over Mount Meron. Douglas will compliment Yolanda on the fabric she's weaving, and Yolanda will praise Douglas for his silver jewelry.

The sun will set (for a change) in the west and Mount Meron go entirely red, like a distant rooster with a comb.

The time has come, Yolanda will say, to turn on the lights, and over the table she'll spread a white tablecloth then go into the kitchen to get dinner ready.

[67]

I've forgotten who the Huguenots were (I think they were French Protestants). But without a doubt they clung to the earth so that Suzy Ortal-Kipnis could study them.

Doctor Ortal-Kipnis—who greets us in the university halls with How are you?—collected documents (at the University of Strasbourg) that shed light (documents that shed light?) on the Huguenot communities in the east of France.

I imagine that there was, at the edge of a document, a Huguenot named Phillip. Perhaps Phillip de Saussüre.

Phillip de Saussüre passed away but Ortal-Kipnis has mentioned his name in an article she sent to a history journal published at Cornell University.

Ortal-Kipnis has pale, tender skin and she wears glasses with golden frames. Since her divorce she's happy and sad.

If only someone (maybe us) would lead Suzy Ortal-Kipnis to the wine cellar next to the Opera House (between Mughrabi Square and the sea) and pour her a glass of Cabernet Sauvignon.

[68]

We don't know why we call the third child by his true name (Yotam). He'll be born only in another five or six years, but *this* decision has already been made.

In the meantime we can tell about Khadra Aloosh, who was injured by our Volkswagen, or about Vassily, the violin teacher (Mikha'el's) who ate an onion while holding his bow.

We went (Yolanda and I and the two children) fishing in the Jordan, and there the thing I've already written of occurred (how the catfish got under the dress).

At times we've skipped a heartbeat (the illness is called, I think, *extra systole*), but the beat that followed was stronger than usual.

We took the sick German shepherd, by way of the desert, to the veterinary hospital in Beer Sheva.

Along the way we saw Bedouin tribes, and the dog, which couldn't breathe (she had a tear in her diaphragm), stuck her head out the window and stared.

[69]

We haven't spoken much of the moon in this

book. One has to understand that the moon is the alter-image of the sun. When the sun lies hidden the moon is revealed, and vice versa.

Without relating to the grammatical dimension of the matter the sun is feminine and the moon masculine, and these things have been determined by virtue of the primordial elements (force versus weakness, and so on). Despite what the physicists think, the moon longs for the sun. As it's waning, it longs with the part that isn't there, even when only a sliver remains.

At the university, all this is considered nonsense. But things take place there that can't be explained by virtue of the university alone. Such as, that a person (whose name is Kaplinski) hangs his coat on a hanger at the entrance to the lecture hall and the coat remains in the same place until the lecture is over.

[70]

Sometimes one sees a line of geese beneath the full moon. One sees the moon. Sees the sky. Beneath

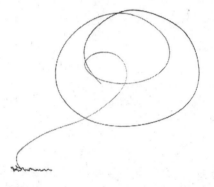

*Sometimes one sees a line of geese beneath the
full moon*

the full moon. The sight and the words (sometimes etcetera) drive us mad.

The entire book is drawn (as things are drawn into a black hole) toward this sentence.

The moon is accidental. It might not have been. We give thanks for the moon. We give thanks for the sky, which isn't to be taken for granted.

Down below we give thanks for each and every goose, and for the ground, for if they didn't tread upon it, they wouldn't be able to walk in a line beneath the moon.

People do not fathom these things. They put cell phones to their ears and shout into them, *Where is Pini?*

On second thought: They too (like the geese) walk beneath the moon. And you too (readers). As the poem has it:

> *The pear-tree in bloom*
> *A woman reads a letter*
> *Beneath the moon*

Not that we need the mercy of heaven. Mercy aplenty we've received beneath the moon. On this earth, here and there, wherever we happen to be found.

[71]

I almost neglected to mention that during these years, Yolanda had a miscarriage. What an awful expression: miscarriage.

Sometimes one is carrying a baby and drops him, and he falls to the floor and in that flash between the hands and floor he's still alive. Sometimes one loses a child because he grows up and now his heart is coarse and his mother seems to him like a walking corpse and he can't wait for her to die.

We (which is to say, I) ask forgiveness from all the women who've miscarried children because they have labored so hard while we have done not a thing.

We should really tell them: In place of the child that was lost, you'll receive a new one. He'll be born without any pain, despite what is said in the ancient curse.

It hasn't occurred to me till now that somewhere,

not far from the Safed Hospital, my dead child is buried.

[72]

The blind mammal that digs tunnels in the ground and is nourished by roots (a mole or mole-rat) came—like the envoys of God that come to cities full of sin—toward our yard in Safed.

If you dig in a place where a small mound has appeared, you've already missed it, since the mammal is, by then, somewhere else just as the present can't be grasped (except as the past).

We've known that we (four mammals) are located *on* the ground, in a stone house, whereas that other mammal (known as *spalax ehrenbergi*) is found *beneath* the ground, and in some strange way it too is added to the deed to the home and to the municipal property tax account.

At that time, more or less, a man named Peretz also came to us. He climbed the stairs, like de Gaulle, in all his glory, and stood before the front door.

He waited there until the door was opened for him (he didn't ring the bell), and then he came in. He said (I recall), "I'm Peretz," and sat on the couch.

What did Peretz want? It was impossible to know. He sat there for maybe twenty minutes, drank tea and ate a few biscuits, then left.

[73]

In 1980 we traveled once again to Japan. Yolanda was already hugging the third child (the baby Yotam), who had been born and—soon after he'd come into the world—raised a fireball over the mountains.

In Anchorage, Alaska, a red light lit up on the airplane's dashboard, and so we sat there, all of us, at the airport, for fifteen hours, in front of a huge stuffed bear.

At the end of October we saw Yolanda looking into a mirror. We wrote a poem (She sprinkles / perfume on the lobe of her ear / my wife of autumn) and we became ill with an inflamed prostate.

At the government hospital in the city of Otsu

(on the shores of a lake called Biwa) a Japanese
man told us that he'd eaten (in Siberia, during the
war) human flesh and we saw urine the color of
gold.

How stupid we are to let the world toss us from
one place to another, while we need to speak to
dentists and poets like warehouse clerks who keep
an account of old equipment (bags here and belts
there) and pile it up on the floor.

What do we remember? The lake at Biwa and
the houses across it. The cherry blossoms and
Auschwitz, Treblinka, Maidenak....

[74]

POEMS THE JAPANESE SAY BEFORE DEATH:
A STUDY (1980–1981)

*I saw the moon / as well and now, world / "Truly
yours ..."*

*Blow, if you will / autumn wind—the flowers /
have all faded*

The surface of the water / reflects / all sorts of things

Fall, plum blossoms, / fall—and leave behind / the memory of fragrance

Oy Mireleh / where have we lost / little Moshe

What are we / doing here? / Is it already morning?

Why have the guards / gone / and what …

From here / one can see / the moon

What kind of tree / did we see on the way / to the crematorium

Did you give / David the bread / Avrum?

Where is Haneleh / I saw her earlier / and now …

Give me back / that prayer book I gave you / yesterday

Hear O Israel / the Lord is our God, the Lord / is one

[75]

The winter of '81 was very cold. Yotam the baby watched Sumo wrestling matches on television all day long and we went to the university library to look for old poems.

On New Year's we pounded rice for the traditional cakes at master Hirano's temple, and we ate sushi during a snowstorm. The ground shook.

In April, when the snow melted, we went (with thirty-six other poets) up to the poet Kyoshi's grave (Alone / I polish lines of a poem, and the sun / is late in setting) and we drank sake until it came time to say the morning prayer.

Imagine that we're in the business of selling doors. Wooden doors. Aluminum doors. Steel doors. And there's a certain very expensive door that's made of bronze.

A man whose name is Ronen (once Krakovski) installs the frames and all evening long we do the books.

If the reader wants a door he'll get a discount

of twenty percent. With the paint job thrown in for free.

[76]

Death is a mute woman. She makes all sorts of muffled sounds and draws the shape of a heart in the air.

Whoever dies in autumn sees the autumn and dies. Whoever dies in spring—the spring. Sometimes the brush slips and falls onto the mat and we find it only after the funeral.

In 1983 Andreas my father wanted to see his brother Ladislaus for the last time.

We pushed him up the stairs (the blood no longer reached his feet) to the second floor, and there, in Uncle Ladislaus's bedroom, they stood facing one another.

Maybe they said *Szervusz* at first, and maybe they said *Szervusz* at the end. At any rate, they spoke Hungarian and it was clear that each of them told a joke.

On the way home, in the Volkswagen, Andreas my

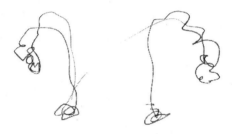

Maybe they said Szervusz at first, and maybe they said Szervusz at the end

father said only, "That's it," and at Rabbi Kook Street (twenty-nine) Ursula, my stepmother, took off his socks and put on a record of Bruckner's string quintet.

[77]

That year (or the year before that) we stood on the pier, in Japan, in front of the Pacific Ocean and between our legs there raced, back and forth, hundreds of crabs.

In Katmandu we saw a female pig and five piglets. And dead rats. The water from the tap was black. A child-god revealed, in exchange for a coin, her face in the window.

In the Philippines we saw mummies. In the city of Bagyo we heard they eat dogs. We bought a black wooden idol, an erect member between his legs.

Sometimes a German man says *oder oder* (or or) but he's mistaken. In fact there are no alternatives. What. Either sky or sea? Wood or earth?

[78]

The man we sat next to on the plane, on the way back home, was born in Barmouth, Wales. There, he said, you lift your hand and you catch a fish in the air. It's enough for the church bells to ring on Sunday and the beach is filled with eels.

In Copenhagen we went to Tivoli Gardens. We went on a giant Ferris wheel and afterward the child Mikha'el got a stomach ache.

Death was in the air there (at Tivoli Gardens) and its scent was the scent of Guinness. You could see people turning into their negatives (as with photographs).

But on the whole we had a good time. We were together there and spoke to one another as though we were not standing on the very thin shell of a very large planet.

[79]

It's a great wonder that the German word for

You could see people turning into their negatives

"darkness" is *Dunkelheit* and that "you" is *du*, as in the Hebrew *du-hayyim* (amphibian).

A man looks at his life in the way that one watches a silent movie. The mouth opens but nothing is heard.

The movements are jumpy, here and there, because the memory film is interrupted by leaps, like quanta in physics.

The horse is here and a moment later there, without having crossed the distance from here to there. But the plot in this Western concerns the heart. The *kokoro*. The *Herz*. The *corazón*.

My mother. Every reader is dear to his mother. She hugs him even from the world of death. His fingernails are hers. His belly is hers. His eyes are hers. Like the great rivers into which smaller rivers flow, so they themselves flow into the sea.

We need to say Thank you. Thank you to the wall for not falling. To the pencil. To the table. To the shopkeeper. To the road. To the radio. To history (with all of its wretched kings). To the old labor union clerks who came from Poland and were beautiful, like Brigitte Bardot.

[80]

If we haven't lost count of the years, we wrote at the time, more or less, a book.

After the great explosion, which can't possibly be imagined, and the stars' freezing over, and the silent journey into infinite darkness, a man is overcome with shame if he writes a book.

And also the days following the creation. Fowl. Mammals. Man. Woman. All that—yes. But a book?

Maybe these things are linked to original sin. By the sweat of your brow shall you eat bread. And you shall see a bird and say *Bird*. See a man and say *Man*. And so, disastrously, a world of signs will cover all things like those enormous sheets in which that nut (what's his name—Christo?) wraps everything.

There should be a law against these things. For instance, a law regarding the sanctity of paper. Or a law relating to the singularity of things (so that they can't be duplicated).

[81]

In any event, not long after we returned to Safed, three cows wandered into the yard. One after another they passed in front of the window and looked into the room and at the desk.

The veterinarian (who was born in Tripoli) came with a rifle that had a syringe in its barrel and he shot them. They also called the cows' owner (one Attias, from the village of Dalton), who said, five or six times: *What am I going to do with them like that?*

In the meantime, night had fallen and the veterinarian had no choice but to go home, and Attias too. We (which is to say, Yolanda and I, and Sivan, Mikha'el, and Yotam) sat on the porch and ate our dinner while the cows lay sleeping on the grass beneath the carob trees.

Most likely they were dreaming of large glass windows beyond which very odd things were happening.

one Attias, from the village of Dalton

Master Hirano came from Japan together with a priest from the Kegon sect and the two of them drank beer all night at the Avia Hotel next to Ben Gurion airport.

The following day, when we came to take them to the Galilee, they had trouble getting up and barely checked out of their rooms on time.

It was a wintry January morning, and near the village of Shefaram the priest from the Kegon sect asked us to stop and stood by the side of the road and urinated.

On Friday the two of them (master Hirano and the priest from the Kegon sect) went to the Bratslav Hasids' synagogue in Safed. The worshippers swayed like trees in the wind. Master Hirano and the priest from the Kegon sect stood there, bald and wrapped in robes, behind the congregation, and the beadle whispered into our ears: *Are they Jews? Are they Jews?*

When we left the synagogue master Hirano said to the priest from the Kegon sect: There is no doubt that they understand what devotion (he said *shujaku*) is. The priest from the Kegon sect said: There is no doubt. They know what devotion is.

On Jerusalem Street, by the monument of the mortar commemorating the '48 war, master Hirano said: Prayer is a good thing. The priest from the Kegon sect said: There is no doubt. Prayer is a good thing.

Master Hirano stood on one side of the mortar and the priest from the Kegon sect stood on the other and the moon rose, big and full, yellow like the fields painted by Van Gogh.

[83]

It's possible to write only by means of non-writing. When things come from the opposite direction.

My aunt Edith rises out of the ground and returns to her bed in the nursing home. Ursula, my stepmother, is walking backward. All sorts of wilted flowers bring their petals toward themselves.

All we need is yoghurt and a spoon. We'll already

know what to do with the spoon. We'll lead it toward the right place (which is to say, the yoghurt) and from there toward the mouth. But the mouth isn't fathomed. Likewise the word that stands for it (mouth) is strange in the extreme.

Or take, for example, the hand that's holding the spoon with its five tragic fingers. There's no logic whatsoever in there being five. Like five widows who've gathered because their husbands have died, allowing themselves this movement through the air in order to keep from losing their minds.

There is no limit to the beauty of things that are sad. Like old clay vases or a wagon's shaft in a junkyard. Every year the plum trees flower anew, and people whose names are Shtiasni or Dahaan open doors and close them.

All these things fill the heart with great joy. The beauty of death and the violet colors accompanying it. Announcements that make nothing dawn on one, and the dawn itself rising from nowhere like a birthday present 365 days a year.

[84]

We came small to this book and now we're big. And we've learned to lie.

For instance, we've seen Professor Pinto at the café in Lisbon, but we haven't seen his dentist, and now we're sending him to the dentist.

We saw a beautiful woman at the ceramic tile shop but we haven't slept with her, and now we're taking her to the hotel next to the ancient Alfama quarter and removing her dress and bra and panties and kneeling on the floor and kissing the soles of her feet and between the toes and her knees and the hair between her legs and her belly and doing to her what all the priests dream of doing on sheets printed with small flowers beneath the forty-watt bulb.

We can perform a de-Hoffmannization of ourselves. In order to become someone else. A fucking expert on stamps sitting in his apartment in Stockholm, and all day saying, *Yoh, Yoh.*

[85]

In Lisbon (in 1988?) we saw a rooster that was tied to an iron anvil but we've already written about that elsewhere, in another book. On the way north (we were driving in an Opel Corsa) we asked how to get out of the city (we'd forgotten its name) going in the direction of Bragança. Someone said that we should take a left and a right. Someone else said we should take a right and a left. We were already far away but the two of them stayed behind for a long time at that spot and argued about the way to Bragança, despite the fact that neither of them had any desire to go there.

Near the city of Braga, on the Atlantic coast, we stood at the edge of a very tall cliff that was known as The End of the World and on clear days (so they said) one could see from there to New York.

There were undoubtedly secret Jews everywhere. You could recognize them by their quasi-Christian appearance. Women dressed in black and men wearing hats were remembering, most likely (from previous generations), the Sabbath rituals.

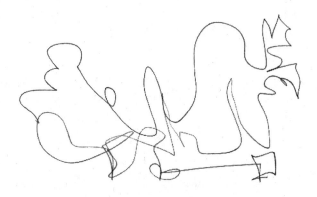

we saw a rooster that was tied to an iron anvil

[86]

In general. Europe consists of two storeys. If you saw thirty women smoking cigarettes at the entrance to a church in Esztergom, Hungary, you could have seen—beneath the heels of their farmers' shoes—the scarves on the heads of the Jewish women.

Or at a rock concert, in Tokai's central square, across from the old prison, you could have heard (from down below—from Hungary's basements) the sound of Jews praying.

Sometimes the earth is full and therefore the dead hover in the air as in Budapest, over the great church. There, around the cross, hundreds of rabbis are standing.

You can, in certain places (principally Poland), do without an umbrella. The Jews who stand between the sky and the city's roofs stop the rain, and when it's very cold, at Christmas, the snow falls on their shtreimels and caftans.

[87]

If you want to tell a story, you'll have to deny the Holocaust.

Imagine for a moment a story that someone is writing in Berlin, about Kurt and Brigitta. Something about an office and difficulties with what they call relationships, and with the subletter they call Yo'akhim, and so on.

Now, unless you introduce red air and red earth into this story, Brigitta and Kurt and Yo'akhim will only be thin lines drawn with a pencil. A shoe lace. A dead centipede. A beetle's case. Dust. Nothing.

Only the blood of the dead can give them life. Therefore Brigitta (even if the story takes place in 1992) is red and Kurt is red, and the air is red, and they need (in the true story) to speak within this air as one might speak under water. For instance, when Kurt says *What did you do yesterday* bubbles of blood emerge from his mouth.

Just as the religious strengthen things by means of the letters *beit-samekh-dalet* ("with God's help"), so they need the red. Their red common market. Their red sky. Let them say: *Guten Blut Morgen* (Good Blood Morning).

It's strange that throughout Europe people strip off their clothes and walk around naked here and there at different times and in different places and not everywhere all at once (as the Jews did).

[88]

In memory of the people in the crematorium, we too are naked. Every time we take off our clothes our bodies are consecrated in their memory, like the parchment in the mezuzah.

Likewise the books we've written are dedicated to them. One explicitly. One allusively. And the others secretly. There isn't a single page from which smoke does not ascend.

Into the books we've gathered the heavenly hosts but we've given them (by the millions) first names. One might say (as they say at dedication ceremonies), we've walked by their light.

Even the electric light bulbs in our homes are taken from there. And the tablecloths, which take the place of shrouds. And especially this air beneath the Shekhinah, the great gust of all that breath *yitgaddal veyitqaddash shemei rabba. be'alma di vra khirutei. veyamlikh malkhutei. veyatzmah purqanei. viqarev meshihei. behayeikhon uveyomeikhon uvehayyei dkhol beit yisrael ba'agala uvizman qariv ve'imru amen. yehei shmei rabba mevorakh le'olam ul'almei almayya. yitbarakh. veyishtabah. veyitpa'ar. veyitromem. veyitnasei. veyithadar. veyitaleh. veyithalal shemei dequdsha brikh hu. Leila min kol-birkhata veshirata. tushbehata venehemata. damiran be'alma ve'imru amen.* (May His great name be exalted and sanctified. In the world which He has established according to His will. And may His kingdom be established. And may His salvation be revealed and His anointed draw near. In your lifetime and in your days. And in the lifetime of all of the house of Israel. Speedily and soon. And say, Amen. May His great name be blessed for all eternity. Blessed. And praised. And glorified. And lifted. And exalted. And extolled. And elevated. And honored be the name of the Holy One blessed be He. Who is beyond all hymns and praise and consolation that might be uttered in this world. And say, Amen.)

[89]

Sometimes places are called *Yad* (meaning a memorial, but literally indicating a hand), like Yad Hannah, and you see a hand cut off (as though by an ax).

If the name is softened by the proximity of a preposition (the hand *of* Hannah), we see the hand still attached to the body and perhaps things around the body.

Likewise the name Bnei Brak is too harsh. It would be better to call the town Bnei Miriam or even Halilyah.

In 1990 more or less, Ursula, my stepmother, decided to send my aunt Edith (who was then eighty-six) to a psychologist.

The psychologist's office was at the Labor Union health clinic on Rabbi Kook Street, number seven (where the Yahalom elementary school's gardens once were and where twice a week we studied agriculture).

Victor Shemesh (who was an insurance agent) took my aunt Edith, who sat in a wheel chair, up to the second floor. He pulled the chair up, step by step, and brought it to a stop in front of the psychologist's door.

We don't know what took place in that room. When she came out (Victor Shemesh waited for her outside and brought her down step by step), my aunt Edith said only: Where's the red bag?

[90]

Andreas my father and my uncle Ladislaus and Aunt Edith have all passed into eternity and most likely they're riding horses there, on the backs of which an address is written (29 Rabbi Kook, etcetera).

It's possible that they've met the great Zionist leader Ussishkin there, and the great Zionist leader Arlozoroff, and the great Zionist leader Smolenskin, but it's hard to imagine them understanding one another.

Out of embarrassment we'll speak of ourselves hyperbolically: The girls selling flowers offered us their bodies and we took them to hotel rooms and made love to them and it's too bad we couldn't have done it in the flowershop.

Secretaries too sought to sleep with us and we obliged them after hours in offices, while the radio played Neil Diamond.

We dreamt about waitresses in cafés, and about nurses in hospitals—as though we were Turks or Croats.

[91]

During those years we also went (as though driven by a certain bipolar disorder) to gatherings of poets.

Correct. Mostly we saw the legs of the female poets but we *truly* wanted to find the right poem, as though we were mathematicians searching for the precise formula for the theory of infinity (which they write out as though they were drawing a worm or snail).

We remember a poet (his name we've forgotten: maybe Barukh Zivtan) who'd posit a thing and then at once negate it. For instance: I walked without my feet and gave her a hand-which-wasn't-a-hand, and so on.

Another poet enlarged small things and made large things smaller, and still another—a woman—wrote an entire series of poems about a barn-owl.

Every so often we'd hear the sounds of artillery fire, coming from the direction of Lebanon, and a man sitting on a bench in front of the Cedars Hotel said (every time those sounds were heard) *yil'an rabkum* (God damn you, in Arabic).

[92]

The child Yotam's heart is large and soft and therefore he takes from the pail the fish we've caught and puts them back in the Jordan River.

Like Anthony of Padova, the Christian, he preaches a sermon to the fish:

"O fish and fish of fish. I am the child who has come into the world through emanation on the one hand and through division on the other, and who gives you life.

Water and air come from the void and return to the void, but the fullness lasts forever, and there is no beauty that compares to that of this body, made of shining silver, which the divine sculptor has fashioned within the waters of the world."

The child Yotam extended his hand before him like the Pope standing on the balcony and blessing the crowds below, and you could see how the sardines were leaping from within the water as though the hands of this child, who was standing on the banks of the Jordan, were a great magnet of compassion.

[93]

The other Anthony (known as the Saint), from Thebes, who lived alone in the desert for one hundred and five years and left it only twice to come to the aid of those who suffered, sought to hold the infant Jesus in his hands just one time before his death, and he was granted that wish, though only in a dream.

And I (Yoel Hoffmann) have held in my hand three infants: Yasmin (who's known here as Sivan) and Tomer (here Mikha'el) and Yotam. Wide awake. By the light of day.

and he was granted that wish, though only in a
dream

How could we possibly give thanks for all this? We can die in order to leave this space to others. Or we can (before we die) drink water in order to mingle the elements within a great perfection. Earth envelops water. Air envelops fire, and all forms (plants, birds, and so on) will be perfect so long as they enter and exit precisely as in a symphony for strings.

Or we can give thanks for these gifts by suddenly hugging a person named Berkowitz at the drugstore, just as he hands the pharmacist a prescription, and say to him: Berkowitz, how great it is that you're here with me.

[94]

In Alexandropolis, Greece, I decided to cross the border to Bulgaria (when was this? I've forgotten) and only an old Bulgarian woman sat with me in the train car. Very few people cross the border there and on that day there were just the two of us. Me and the old Bulgarian woman.

The Bulgarian woman had some thirty large paper bags and already at the Alexandropolis station I found myself helping her load them onto the train. The old Bulgarian woman laughed in my direction with a toothless mouth and out of one of the bags she took two bottles of red wine and a package of sugar.

We talked all the way to Bulgaria. I don't speak Bulgarian, and she didn't speak any of the other languages, and so we spoke without words, helped by gestures we made with our hands, about everything under the sun.

She'd already finished a fifth bottle (she made me drink as well, maybe a bottle and a half) and half a package of sugar (the sugar she'd cup in her hand) by the time the train stopped at the border.

There we were ordered to present all of our belongings for inspection. I had a single suitcase—and the Bulgarian woman had her thirty bags.

The customs officers let me go without delay, but they huddled around the old lady and took out everything she had in the bags and, on a long table, piled up cans of food, bottles of wine, bottles of oil, packets of tea, jars of coffee, etcetera. All the while the old lady was tugging at my shirt sleeve as she shouted and wept.

Through the window of the hut I saw the train continuing on its way to Bulgaria while I was still in the firm grip of the old woman.

The deliberations and discussions between the officers and the old lady went on through the night, and finally we put all the cans and the bottles and the other items back into the paper bags and took the bags out onto a bench by the tracks. There, on the bench, the two of us sat until morning, when another train came, it too almost completely empty.

We carried the thirty bags onto the train and again we sat and drank red wine until we reached Sofia.

I could have stepped out of my life and gone with her. And lived in an old apartment building in a suburb of Sofia, and crossed the border to Alexandropolis, in Greece, once a month and made god-knows-what profit from the differences in price between the two countries.

I almost spoke Bulgarian. I almost had a mother and grandmother of my own. We could have shared the wine and the sugar for another four or five years, but I was afraid she'd die (her veins were already swollen and her lips were purple) and leave me there all alone.

[95]

So that's how it is. Some philosophers think that the world depends on consciousness. The radicals among them say that in fact it *is* that (the world *is* consciousness).

Professor Yehoyakhin Shoval is of this opinion. Sometimes we meet in the hall and greet one another with *How are you,* or even have salmon and rice with vegetables together in the cafeteria (Professor Shoval generally prefers chicken thighs).

Lately Professor Shoval has been speaking before advanced students on the topic: "Is Davidson an epiphenomenalist?" We (which is to say, I) had not heard of Davidson until that day. An epiphenomenalist is (in short, so as not to weary the reader) a man who believes that consciousness is like the vapor that rises off of soup (if the body is the soup).

There is a dark side to Professor Shoval's life. Things have happened that are better not spoken

There is a dark side to Professor Shoval's life

of, but the rest of his life (maybe ninety-five per-cent) is on the whole filled with light.

The world is in fact consciousness and when we close our eyes it disappears, apart (if we're lucky) from the woman who touches us from time to time, if she's having a bad dream.

[96]

We like the song that Louis Armstrong sings with Ella Fitzgerald about the sycamore tree. We don't know what sort of tree that is, but when we hear the song the heart begins to travel far. To Abyssinia. Where the plains seem to be painted turquoise and gazelles leap in slow motion over the horizon.

To Formosa. Whales come up onto the beach there and sometimes (as in the movie "The Piano") an organ rises up from the depths.

Or, the heart goes out to the future, which is also a kind of shore, and sirens (not alarms, but women whose voices are irresistible) sing there and seduce the sailors.

Or to the past, where mothers so beautiful it's painful hug an infant and a man emerges from a carpentry shop and says: It doesn't matter if the baby's not mine.

This song ("Dream a Little Dream of Me") is the song of the book and every reader should listen to it on a loop (which is to say, from beginning to end to beginning again an infinite number of times) so that we won't go wrong like Leonardo da Vinci, whose entire life was taken up with drawing sketches of complex catapults and all sorts of other contraptions.

[97]

Maybe ten years before the end of the second millennium my son Yotam came back from school and behind him walked a Great Pyrenees.

The dog lay down in the yard (where, some ten years earlier, the three cows had lain) for two days and looked toward Mount Meron. And now I want to send him a kind of text message wherever he is today (most likely the Eden of dogs):

Thank you for allowing my soul to come so close to yours. There are things that only the two of us know. Things that are impossible to say because words are made of materials resembling cut sheets of tin and man doesn't have the tools to bring great spirit into them.

But since you were willing to look at me (for a moment) with those eyes of yours two or perhaps three times I knew something that you knew—something immeasurably more profound than these thoughts of mine and than the great river of memories that we call life.

[98]

How can it be that entire mountains, continents, and stars are found within the skull?

The food market in the city of Tainan (Taiwan) is there. The black hens. Pig corpses. The hunchbacked fishmonger.

Pictures of hell from Taoist temples are found in the skull. A priest coming out of the temple (in the skull) kicks a rat and rides away on a Vespa. The Long Spring Hotel in the city of Ma-kung is found there in its entirety—all six floors—within the skull. The city's coral salesmen. What isn't there?

The whores in the capital city Taipei. The mausoleum holding Chiang Kai-shek's body. All these are within the skull.

We are within the skull. And so is the skull itself.

[99]

I'm having a dream: a string on which pearls are strung is snapped (from whose neck had the necklace hung?) and an infinite number of pearls scatter across the floor.

Beneath the chairs and under the bed and the closet I gather them up one by one. But how many can I gather? At most a hundred.

[100]

Better to sleep. The night's first name is Pardon. And its ancient symbol—white sheets.

The trees' roots embrace the ribs of those

beneath the ground, and above, crows call out the letters of prayers that appear in the great hymnal.

Everything grows increasingly distant. Only the women linger, like those lights one sees along the horizon, during the winter night at the Pole.